THE SON
OF THE SLIME
WHO ATE CLEVELAND

THE SON
OF THE SLIME
WHO ATE CLEVELAND

Marjorie Weinman Sharmat

Illustrated by Rodney Pate

A YEARLING BOOK

Published by
Dell Publishing Co., Inc.
1 Dag Hammarskjold Plaza
New York, New York 10017

Yearling ® TM 913705, Dell Publishing Co., Inc.

ISBN: 0-440-48086-8

Printed in the United States of America
First printing—November 1985

CW

For Frank Kalil,
who knows what friendship really means

Belongs to:

Vivian Hanna or

Hanna Family

Chapter 1

My name is Frank, and I'm planning to fly to school today. Or maybe crawl underground. Or perhaps go as The Invisible Boy. I can't go to school the usual way because Jack and Lee might be waiting for me. Waiting to get me.

Not too long ago the three of us were good friends. We hung around together so much that we were called The Sticky Three. But a few weeks ago Jack and Lee got into what might be called The Jelly Bean Challenge. It wasn't much of anything, but I told a few people about it. Well, to be Perfectly Frank, which I always am, I told the entire city about it. And then it wasn't little anymore. Sometimes I do things that kids with no imagination might say are a bit weird. Some kids have minds that go straight ahead, no detours, no side trips, no sense of adventure. But not me, Frank.

I wasn't looking for adventure the afternoon it all began. I was just looking to stay awake. The three of us were at Lee's house, and Jack and Lee were talking about how to make a million dollars, and things like that. They're sort of competitive. When Lee said, "I'm going to make a million dollars someday," Jack said, "I'm going to make two million."

"Three for me," said Lee.

"Four," said Jack.

I always try to stay out of these conversations. I plan to be in show business when I grow up, and in show business you can make ten million fast or starve fast. Jack is planning to be a lawyer, and Lee wants to be a banker. Jack got his idea for being a lawyer by watching all those legal TV shows. Lee's mother always lets him hold the money when they're in a bank, and I guess it feels good to Lee. He was only two years old when he got his first withdrawal and deposit slips.

I get bored with all their figures, and by the time they reached fifteen million dollars that afternoon, I was yawning. But they ignored me. Lee got a couple of pieces of paper, and he and Jack started to write things down. Statistics. Figures. Games with numbers. They were getting rich on paper and I was falling asleep.

"The easiest way to get rich is by using your head," Jack said.

But once they used mine. They each estimated how many hairs I had on my head and then they counted them. Pulling and yanking. It was awful. They were

10

both way off in their estimates. My head was sore for days, but I'm a friend, right?

I yawned again and headed for the door. "I'm going down to the mall and buy a record," I said. "You two just stay here and count your billions."

But Lee said, "I'll go with you, Frank. I want to see what's new at the computer store."

"Me too," said Jack.

They threw their papers into a wastebasket. Just like that, plans for making millions and millions of dollars tossed away. But I knew they would build new financial empires the next day.

It was a nice walk to the mall. Nobody mentioned figures, statistics, boring things like that. I like to dream and scheme, too, but I follow everything up with action. Adventure. Like once I got hold of a baby picture of Lee and I tacked it up on the bulletin board at school with a sign *Guess Who*. A teacher took it down almost immediately just because Lee wasn't wearing anything. Anything at all. But Lee and some kids saw it first. Lee pretended he was just staring at the tacks.

Then once I sent a mushy letter to Jack and signed it *Your Secret Admirer*. The secret admirer asked Jack to come to a certain bench at school. And Jack showed up. And I showed up with a Your Secret Admirer sign. Jack pretended he was just there to dust the bench slats.

To be Perfectly Frank, I'd rather do things like that than make a million dollars. I want to express myself. I want to talk, sing, shout, be a part of everything that's going on. I don't want to go through life just breathing and eating and being on the sidelines.

11

We got to the mall. Jack said, "I wonder what crazy things are going on here today."

There are always crazy things going on in the mall. But one of them, in its multicolored icky splendor, was just lying in wait for The Sticky Three.

Chapter 2

A gigantic jar of jelly beans was sitting above a sign that said HOW MANY JELLYBEANS IN THE JAR? GUESS RIGHT AND WIN TWO TICKETS TO MONSTER MAYHEM, NOW PLAY-ING AT THE MERRY MIDTOWN MALL THEATRE, AND ALL THE JELLYBEANS YOU CAN EAT IN TWO HOURS.

A lady was sitting next to the jar, and she was hand-ing out entry blanks. She had a big stack of them in front of her on a table. When she saw Jack, Lee, and me she said, "Would you like to enter the contest?"

The lady had the kind of voice that sounds like it's wearing glasses. I wondered how she felt when she got up in the morning and knew she would have to spend her entire day sitting beside a gigantic jar of jelly beans.

A sign on the table said that the contest was being sponsored by Radio Station KNIF. I listen to music on it a lot. It drives my parents nuts.

"Boring contest," I said. "Counting all that stuff."
The lady gave me a dirty look.

"Sorry," I said. "I'm just not a counter. For a counter, I'm sure this is a very interesting contest."

She gave me another dirty look.

"Jelly beans and movie tickets," said Jack. "What kind of prize is that?"

I was beginning to feel Perfectly Frank. I said, "Jelly beans aren't the best kind of prize. A person could get ill on jelly beans. Why don't you have nice healthy raw vegetables for a prize? Carrots, celery, stuff like that."

"Vegetables?" The lady's voice took off its glasses. She was getting teed off at us.

"Honestly. If there were more prizes of vegetables, people would get the idea that vegetables are something good to have. I'm just telling you what I think."

Jack tugged at my arm. "She's not interested in what you think, Frank. This is a jelly bean contest, not a vegetable stand."

"You haven't got it quite right either, young man." The lady was talking to Jack. "This contest is a mathematical challenge. If you don't see it that way, then this contest isn't for you."

"Jelly beans in a jar are a mathematical challenge?" Jack scratched his head.

"Could be," said Lee.

"Oh, c'mon," I said. "The record store will close."

Jack and Lee took one last look at the jar of jelly beans. Then they shrugged and followed me to the record store. They stood around while I bought a record that they both hoped they'd never have to listen to. They both like classical music, and they always wear

14

clean socks, which I mention together because I think one is connected to the other.

Then we went to the computer store. Nobody treats us with respect in the computer store because we don't have enough money to buy a computer. Record stores are much better. There wasn't anything new to see in the store because Jack and Lee had been there just the day before.

On the way out of the mall we passed the gigantic jar of jelly beans again. People were actually lining up to enter the contest. Maybe they were hungry.

Jack stopped and looked at the jar.

So did Lee.

Then I heard, "Six, six, six, six." Like a chant. Lee and Jack seemed to be chanting together. I don't know who started first, but it was like a duet.

I said, "What?"

They both said, "Six thousand six hundred and sixty-six."

"Wait a minute. This is a conspiracy," I said. "You both decided together that there are six thousand six hundred sixty-six jelly beans in that jar?"

"Separately," said Jack. "I decided first. I took one look at the circumference of that jar and the angles of the jelly beans, and I computed on the spot."

"No, *I* did," said Lee. "I even said it out loud. Six thousand six hundred sixty-six on the button." Lee was sounding like a banker counting money.

"No, I said it first," said Jack as he looked at me. Suddenly I was the judge.

"Look," I said, "there are three thousand one jelly beans in that jar. Believe me."

I couldn't think of a reason in the world why they should believe me. But it sounded like a good thing to say.

The jelly bean lady was listening to us. "The three of you are entering the contest?"

"I am," I said.

I hoped that would stop Jack and Lee. They wouldn't want to enter a contest with an amateur counter like me.

The lady handed me a pen and an entry blank. I filled in my name, address and telephone number in the right places. I also printed the word *yes* after the question *Are you a regular listener to Station KNIF?* I wanted to add *except when I'm in school,* but there wasn't any room. Then I printed 3,001 after the question *How many jelly beans in the jar?* I put my entry in a slot in a box on the table.

Jack and Lee took entry blanks and filled them out. They were entering even though I had. I couldn't see what they wrote down. The lady smiled as they stuck their entries in the slot. I asked her, "What happens if nobody guesses right?"

"The person who comes closest to the correct number will win."

"Sounds fair," I said.

On the way home from the mall I said, "That jelly bean contest is really dumb. I'm going to be proud when I lose it. I mean, think how embarrassing it would be to *win.* Like you're the jelly bean king or something."

Jack laughed. "Okay," he said. "I'll be proud to lose it."

"Count me in," said Lee. "The Sticky Three Losers."

We laughed all the way to my house where I made them listen to my new record. I figured the contest was over.

But the next day at school I was, as usual, Perfectly Frank. I told Blitz Melnick about the contest and how Jack and Lee both claimed they thought of 6,666 first. I also told a couple of teachers. And three girls in the lunchroom. Two guys in assembly. The maintenance man sweeping up the halls.

It was just a small local contest, but when I talked about it, it seemed to get bigger. And more interesting. And more competitive between Jack and Lee. The last person I told was Bianca Wasserman, who was interested in anything I could tell her about Jack and Lee. "If I change my name to 6,666 will they compete over me?" she asked.

She expected an answer. For once I was speechless.

I was walking home from school when a kid at a bus stop told *me* about the contest. He said that Jack and Lee were competing for a $6,666 prize and a trip to Europe.

I thanked him for the information. I saw Jack and Lee behind me and they looked kind of determined. I started to walk fast. They caught up with me. Jack grabbed me and said, "Frank Kalpal, how come you didn't get a loudspeaker and make an announcement to the whole school?"

"I didn't think of it," I said.

Chapter 3

Everything might have quieted down and fizzled out if only Bianca Wasserman hadn't had her party!

Bianca Wasserman was always having parties. Her family is rich and her house is enormous. Her parents, Doctors Glinka and Max Wasserman, are both psychologists who thought it was healthy for kids to make a wreck out of a house. "Aggression-wise, it makes good sense for kids," her mother says. "Otherwise they might grow up to rob convenience stores."

What can I say about Bianca Wasserman? She has two huge front teeth that cause her to look as if she's smiling whether she is or not, and her hobby was making phony phone calls. She made most of them to Jack.

I was at Jack's house when she telephoned and invited him to the party. Jack's parents have a telephone amplifier system, so you can hear the voice of anyone who telephones even if you're in another room. The system does other things, too. Jack was fooling around with it when I got to his house. "I could have a legal conference simultaneously with Hong Kong, Athens, and London," he said. "This will be great for my law office."

"What law office?"

"The one I'll get when I'm a lawyer. Just like on TV. I'll have lots of windows, thick carpets, and plants that never die. I'll buy a picture of a family and put it on my desk. It makes a good impression to have a picture of your family on your desk. A dog helps a lot too. Cocker spaniels. They're the best. Friendly-looking ears. And a hobby, so that clients who come in don't think that all I'm interested in is the law. But I have to have a hobby I can put on a wall. Can you think of a good wall hobby?"

"I hope not."

"In place of a wall hobby, I can have photographs taken of myself with politicians. But that can be dangerous. One minute a politician is up, the next minute he's down. If I'm in a picture with him then I go up and down with him."

The telephone rang. "London calling," I said.

Jack picked up the receiver. "Hello."

The voice on the other end sounded as if it were in a recording studio. That's what the amplification system does. "Hello," said the voice. "This is your friendly dognapping service calling to inquire whether you have any dogs to kidnap. We have a money-saving offer today. Two dogs for the price of one. Additional charge for dogs over seventy-five pounds or four feet in height."

"Hello, Bianca."

"How do you know it's me?"

"Lucky guess."

Bianca's giggles were amplified all over the house.

"So how about the dognapping offer?"

"I don't own a dog."

"Well, my offer also applies to cats and goldfish."

More giggles.

Jack looked at me. Then he turned off the amplifier switch. He didn't want me to hear the conversation. I went to the living room and turned on the TV. They kept talking.

I was beginning to get the idea that Jack liked these telephone calls. Could he actually *like* Bianca? Aside from the phony phone calls and the giggles and her parents and her teeth and a few other things I haven't mentioned, she wasn't bad.

Jack came into the living room. "She invited me to a party," he said. "It's a costume party. She's asking everyone to come as their favorite monster."

"That sounds like Bianca."

"What do you mean? Bianca's okay."

I was right. He *did* like Bianca.

"So you're going," I said. "Who's your favorite monster?"

"A judge who sentenced someone to twenty years for stealing a jelly doughnut."

"I should have known."

When I got home, my mother told me that Bianca had called to invite me to a party. I called Bianca back and said yes. I guess I was in the mood to be a werewolf.

I went to the party with Jack and Lee. Lee was dressed as a famous New York banker who embezzled $133,842,572.99 and was on his way to Brazil. Jack was dressed in a long black robe and he was carrying a gavel.

Bianca's parents greeted us at the door. They were wearing identical moldy green costumes. "We're Mr. and Mrs. Slime Who Ate Cleveland," they announced.

The Wassermans always butted into Bianca's parties. "Shared" is how they put it.

Bianca rushed over. She was wearing something that had a long snout, under which her two front teeth gleamed menacingly. "I'm so glad you could come," she said to Jack, Lee, and me. She looked at Jack.

Bianca stood there with her long snout, her two front teeth, and her parents beside her proudly looking like slime. It was a fantastic family portrait. If only I had a camera. I could probably sell the picture to one of those junky newspapers you see at supermarket checkout counters. PSYCHOLOGISTS AND DAUGHTER EXPERIENCE UNEXPLAINABLE PHENOMENON. TURN INTO MONSTERS. DIABOLICAL PLOT AGAINST WASSERMAN FAMILY SUSPECTED.

Almost every kid at the party was Dracula or a pirate. But some were dressed as heroes and colorful historical figures. Not everybody wants to be a monster. I had trouble becoming a werewolf, but my mother helped me.

There was plenty of food, which is why most of the kids went to Bianca's parties. You were also allowed to

stand on sofas, tables, and chairs, spill soda, and scream. I think her parents are crazy.

Bianca's mother cheered them on. "Expend that energy, kids!" she said. "Let it all hang out."

If my parents knew what went on at the Wasserman house, they'd never let me go to Bianca's parties. My parents are quiet and sane. Most kids my age really don't want to walk on sofas or coffee tables. They want freedom, but not that much.

Bianca was hanging around Jack, and Lee went to get some food, so I walked around by myself. Bianca's father followed me. He wears thick glasses and he's very thin and he looks as if he's never eaten anything, let alone Cleveland.

"You're not mixing," he said. "You should mingle with the other guests."

"Well, I'm kind of looking around."

"If you start out as a loner, you could grow up alienated. Do you know what group is responsible for most of the assassinations in the world?"

"Well . . ."

"It's the alienated. The poor slob who lives alone or perhaps with a few cockroaches in his cold-water apartment, eating stale sandwiches, drinking beer, and dreaming his distorted dreams of glory."

"Oh well, I guess that's a good piece of information to have, but my dreams of glory are to succeed in show business and—"

"Show business? Have you had career counseling, son?"

Son? He called me son. I was The Son of The Slime Who Ate Cleveland!

No way! It was time to be Perfectly Frank.

"Dr. Slime," I began. "I mean Dr. Wasserman. Just for openers, I'm not your son."

"Well, of course you're not, in actual fact. But I feel I can guide you, in a paternal sort of way, to be the person you want to be. Let's say I've adopted you intellectually and vocationally."

"Let's say you haven't."

Dr. Wasserman smiled a greenish smile.

I wasn't through talking. "Right now *your* vocation is being a slime and eating Cleveland. If I'm supposed to be your son, that isn't much of a role model."

"Son, may I remind you that you're presently a werewolf."

I looked around the room. Why was this happening to me and not to Jack or Lee? What was it about me that got me into situations like this? Maybe I should be proud to get singled out. I looked at Dr. Wasserman, still smiling greenly, and I didn't feel proud.

He stood up. "What you need is group activity. It assimilates the loners."

Dr. Wasserman adjusted his glasses and walked over to his wife. I saw him pointing at me and kind of shaking his head sadly. Then his wife shook her slimy green head sadly. They whispered together for a while and then they both nodded their slimy green heads up and down. Have you ever had two monsters consulting over you? Dr. Glinka Wasserman tapped on a table. "Listen, everybody. We are going to have a potato-sack race across the living room. Won't that be fun?"

"No!" said Jack. "It won't be fun. It's okay at picnics, but it's dumb in a living room."

25

Everybody turned and looked at Jack.

Lee stopped eating. I knew he would agree with Jack, and I was glad. Somebody had to stop the Wassermans.

"A potato-sack race across the living room sounds great to me," said Lee.

Maybe Lee was bored with the party, but *that* bored?

"No, it's dumb," said Jack. "I'm going to be a lawyer, and that's how I know. If you went into a court of law and asked a jury to decide whether or not it's dumb, it would take twelve people five minutes to decide yes. And that's counting the time it takes to get in and out of the jury box and maybe stop off at the bathroom."

"Well, I'm going to be a banker someday," said Lee.

"So what's that got to do with this?" asked Jack.

"I might lend money to people who want to invest in potato sacks. We have to keep the economy moving."

"In potato sacks, across the living room?" asked Jack.

I piped up. "Let's have a potato-counting contest."

I figured that would stop the potato-sack debate.

Bianca squealed, "WHEEeee, like that jelly bean–counting contest in the mall! The one that Jack and Lee are fighting over."

"*Fighting* over? Who told you that?" I asked.

"You told me," said Bianca. "Don't you remember?"

"I didn't say *that*. I didn't use those words. Maybe a hot and heavy competition—"

"Hey, everybody," Bianca yelled. "How many of you think Jack guessed 6,666 jelly beans first? How many of you think Lee guessed 6,666 first? Vote, vote!"

The jelly bean business was growing like a weed that was out of control. Unfortunately I was the one who

26

had planted it, watered it, and kept it thriving. Me, Perfectly Frank, gardener.

Lee got eight votes. Jack got six. The day after the party, Bianca Wasserman switched her phony phone calls to Lee, the winner.

Chapter 4

Bianca Wasserman was turning Lee into a telephone coward. "I can't answer it. It might be her again. And again," he said to me two days after the party. Bianca had called him six times in a day and a half.

We were sitting in Lee's room. "The phone isn't ringing," I said. "It's nice and peaceful. You have a tranquil telephone, Lee. The bells are ringing in your head."

"It will ring," he said. "How did I get into this? Now she's after me instead of Jack. I think he hexed her on me. That's his jelly bean revenge. Would you want to go through life never being able to answer the telephone?"

I kept quiet. I didn't want to admit that I was also afraid to answer the telephone ever since the party. I was afraid that Father Slime Wasserman was going to phone me, his intellectually and vocationally adopted son, with more advice. But I hadn't heard from him. Maybe an intellectual-vocational-type adoption doesn't require father and son to keep in close touch. I hoped I was free of him. Maybe I could offer myself up as a telephone answering sacrifice to Bianca Wasserman so she'd lay off Jack and Lee. I, Perfectly Frank, was willing to do anything for my pals.

But a day later, Jack and Lee were as friendly as ever. However, they had a few words for me. "Frank," said Lee, "the contest is a big deal because *you* made it a big deal. I'm not going to win and Jack isn't going to win. So stop talking jelly beans! Could you do that for Jack and me?"

"I could try. Are you two mad at me?"

"No."

"No."

Jack and Lee hardly ever got mad at me. I figured I could go on forever just being myself. And maybe I could have if that jar of jelly beans hadn't done me in.

One afternoon after school I turned on my radio as usual. To Station KNIF of course. I was listening to music when suddenly an announcer roared, "We have a jelly bean winner!" Boy, was he dramatic. I personally would never trust anybody who acts as if jelly beans are the ultimate excitement.

The voice went on to say, "Actually we have *two* winners in our How Many Jelly beans in the Jar? contest held recently at Merry Midtown Mall. And I won't keep you in suspense a moment longer. The correct number of jelly beans in the jar was six thousand nine hundred and thirty-one!"

The announcer seemed to think this was very good news. I thought it was too. It meant that neither Jack nor Lee had won. Now we could all forget that jelly bean business.

The announcer went on. "No one guessed six thousand nine hundred thirty-one. *But,* the closest to that figure was six thousand six hundred sixty-six, a number submitted by a Mr. Jack Redtress and a Mr. Lee Goodfellow. So, guys, you are *both* winners, and you'll split the prize. You will each receive one ticket to *Monster Mayhem,* now playing on the wide screen at the Merry Midtown Mall Theatre, plus all the jelly beans each of you can eat in one hour. Congratulations!"

"No! How can you do that to my friends!" I yelled at the voice on the radio. "*Lose* is what they have to do. *Lose,* do you hear me?"

But the radio station was already back to playing music.

The news got around the school fast. Some kids congratulated Lee on winning. Some kids congratulated Jack. It was like taking sides. I was smart. *I* knew the right thing to say.

I saw Jack first. I said, "Congratulations. Where's the *other* winner?"

"The *other* winner?" said Jack. "That 6,666 was mine! I calculated it first."

"You were *both* winners," I said. "What could you do with two tickets to that terrible movie anyway. And *two* hours of all the jelly beans you can eat—*yecchh!* Did you know that four dentists and six nutrition groups made a protest about that prize?"

I saw Lee coming toward us. But when he saw us, he

started to walk away. "Hey, Lee," I yelled, and I grabbed him with one hand. I had already grabbed Jack with the other.

"This is silly," I said. "Remember what good friends you are and have been and will be forever."

Jack and Lee just glared at each other.

"Let's forget the contest. Do it for *me*, your old pal Frank. Just as a little favor. Think of everything I've done for *you*."

Suddenly I thought of the naked baby picture and the Your Secret Admirer sign. "Okay, so don't think of everything I've done for you. Just think how dumb it is to get mad over 6,666. A really nothing number. It's so boring and repetitive, I could fall asleep saying 6,666."

I was going to yawn, but Jack and Lee had already walked away. In opposite directions.

Chapter 5

I have an ally at school. Someone who's always on my side. Unfortunately. Ms. Pillsbury, my teacher, thinks I'm great. I wish she would think it silently. But she compliments me in front of the other kids. Some of them hoot, some of them give me sly looks, and some of them wait until after class and then kid me.

After my unsuccessful try at getting Jack and Lee to be pals again, I went to Ms. Pillsbury's class. We were studying history that morning. I sat in back, as usual. Lee and Jack were in the row in front of me, and so was Lemon Derringer, a girl I personally would have named Lemon if her parents hadn't beat me to it. Blitz Melnick, the class troublemaker, sat down beside me.

Ms. Pillsbury stood behind her desk, full of authority in her orthopedic shoes. Her hair was always braided resolutely across her head and her clothes looked like they were uniforms from a disbanded army. She wanted us to know this was a no-nonsense class. We knew.

"Children," she began. Everyone flinched.

"I've been looking over the results of your latest test. Would you like me to share them with you?"

A few kids shook their heads no.

"Most of you descended into the basement of your mentality. Are you following me?"

More head shakes.

"You *flunked*!" said Ms. Pillsbury. "Now is that clear?"

Everyone nodded yes.

"Not everyone flunked," said Ms. Pillsbury. "Lemon Derringer did very well. And Frank Kalpal got an A plus. The only A plus in the class."

"Frank's not in the basement of his mentality," said Blitz Melnick. "How about that!"

Everyone started to hoot.

Ms. Pillsbury was angry. "Stop that! You know, I didn't *have* to be a teacher. No one dragged me kicking and screaming into this classroom. I suspect that's how most of you got here. At your age going to school is not a voluntary act. You *have* to be here. Are we all agreed on that?"

The class mumbled yes.

"*I* could have become a ballet dancer or an architect. But I chose teaching because there is nothing in this world more important than young minds."

Ms. Pillsbury turned and wrote *young minds* on the blackboard. "Please repeat after me: *young minds*."

The class mumbled young minds or wong rinds or lung kinds or something like that.

"Good," said Ms. Pillsbury. "I sense we're communi-

34

cating. Now for tonight's homework assignment, I'm going to challenge all of your young minds. I want you to write an essay of not more than five hundred words explaining how one of the major or minor wars of history could have been avoided. Choose your own war. It can be a famous or an obscure war."

"If we don't know of a war, can we make one up?" asked Blitz. Blitz never bothered to raise his hand.

"You mean you've never heard of *any* war? Not one war comes to mind? I can't believe you've come so far in school with so little knowledge. You should be familiar with at least ten wars by the time you reach fifth grade."

"I'll lend you the Revolutionary War, Blitz," said Lemon. "I don't need it. I've got the Civil."

"My mother and father fight. Does that count?" asked Blitz.

I raised my hand. It shot up without my permission. But there it was! Was this my chance to do something about Jack and Lee? Maybe we could have a class discussion on the subject of friendships. What did this have to do with history? Plenty. War, peace, battles, treaties, amnesty, they all boiled down to friendship, or lack of it. Jack and Lee would have to listen. They were stuck in this class.

"Yes, Frank?" Ms. Pillsbury was waiting.

"Sometimes wars begin with little fights. Like between two kids."

Jack and Lee turned and tried to stare me down.

"Are you saying that two children could start a full-scale war?" asked Ms. Pillsbury.

"Well, no. But it's a beginning."

35

"You mean like this?" asked Blitz, and he leaned over and pushed my books off my desk. They landed on the floor. Bianca Wasserman, who might be second in line for class troublemaker, pushed the books of the kid beside her.

Someone shouted, "War!" and books started to drop to the floor.

"Children!" screamed Ms. Pillsbury. "There will be no wars in this class! In fact, the subject is closed. Return all books to all desks immediately."

I raised my hand. "But I have some important things to say."

"Later, Frank. In about twenty years. When all of these children have grown up." Ms. Pillsbury sighed. "Long ago I divided this class into categories. There are those who sail paper airplanes. There are those who fall asleep. There are those who mistake this for a lunchroom and entertain us with the crackling of potato chips and the slurping of milk. There are those who think they are Superman and would like to install a telephone booth, change their clothes at will, and zoom off, never to return. And then there is a straggly group, pitifully small in number, who earnestly wish to *learn*. This tiny contingent is headed, as we all know, by you, Frank."

The class exploded. Ms. Pillsbury stamped her othopedic shoe.

"Listen, all of you," she said. "It's terribly lonely being a genius. You should be more understanding."

That did it! Ms. Pillsbury did not understand that there is a right way and a wrong way to deal with

36

genius. You don't toss the word around in a classroom overrun by certifiable noodleheads.

Lee and Jack turned around and smirked at me. I wanted to leave the classroom and never return. Never! Unless I could join the paper airplanes group, the sleepers, the Superman group, the eaters, or the slurpers.

But I would rise again. With a real plan to get my pals back together again. No more classroom discussions for Perfectly Frank. *Action* was needed. And ingenuity. And raw guts. My specialties.

Chapter 6

You have to pay a price for having unusual ideas, for being different, for being Perfectly Frank. My price has been following me around for years. Lemon Derringer.

Lemon Derringer is a girl who got on my trail in kindergarten and never gave up. She has been watching me all this time, waiting for me to make The Big Mistake. She has two favorite words, *I'm telling*. And she tells. She carries tales about me to Mr. Sklish, our principal. "I saw Frank do this, I saw Frank do that."

And Mr. Sklish always tells her, "Proof, I need proof, my dear Lemon."

Lemon doesn't have any proof. At least not yet. Whenever she catches me doing something, she goes straight to Mr. Sklish, who sends her on her way with his all-time favorite password, *Proof!* Then she writes me a little note, *I know what you did. Sincerely, Lemon Derringer.* I have fourteen notes.

I don't think I could ever play a trick on anyone that would equal the trick her parents played on her by naming her Lemon. That's her absolutely real official name. Her parents thought she was sunny and bright and so they named her Lemon. They could have named her Sunshine, which is terrible but better.

"Hey, Frank."

Lemon was calling to me.

"You haven't done anything nutsy in a couple of weeks. How come? Are you sick?"

"I never do anything nutsy."

Lemon put her face right next to mine. "I'm gonna get you next time. This is my year. The year of Lemon Derringer."

"Don't you ever give up?"

"I can read your face. It tells me you're planning something very big soon. Your face says major, colossal, stupendous. Oh, I get so excited when I see *colossal* on your face!"

Lemon walked away.

Was she right? Did I have *colossal* written on my face? After my disaster in the classroom, I knew I had to be careful about my next step. But if it turned out to be major, colossal, and stupendous, well, those are the breaks!

Chapter 7

When I got home from school I thought about sending an anonymous note to Ms. Pillsbury, telling her that genius is not a public-announcement word but a sort of ripped-underwear word, to be spoken of privately, quietly. I would tell her that I represent a large percentage of the world's geniuses and we're all in agreement on this matter. I would sign it *Member of Geniuses Anonymous.*

Then I wondered if sending this note on the same day she had called *me* a genius represented very bad timing on my part.

The telephone rang. Could it be Ms. Pillsbury apologizing? No. People like Ms. Pillsbury don't apologize. They just take deep breaths, regroup their thoughts, and charge forward again on their orthopedic shoes.

I answered the phone. "Hello. This is not an answering machine. This is a real person. However, if you are selling something, please hang up. We have two of everything we need."

My parents gave me permission to answer the telephone this way. Sometimes I just say hello. It depends on how I feel.

"I *knew* you wouldn't just say hello," said the voice on the other end of the line. It was a man's voice. I didn't recognize it.

"How could you know how I would answer the phone? Have you called me before?"

"No, but I know how your mind works, son."

Son. It was The Slime Who Ate Cleveland! He was calling me up, dialing my number with his scaly green claws. He went on. "It's your mind that I want to talk about, son. We were having such an interesting conversation the other night, but we never finished it. I want to get back to it. Son, you'll be wasting your mind if you go into show business. Do you know what show business is all about?"

"Fame, money, applause, limos . . ."

"Rejection, son! The most horrible thing on earth. I'm a psychologist, you know, and my waiting room is full of people suffering from rejection. Can you guess what's paid for my big house, my thick rugs, my Cadillac, my life-style? Rejection, that's what."

"Well, I'm glad they're all paid for."

"That's not the point. The point is that a boy with your intelligence should aim higher than you're aiming. I'd like to talk about that with you and give you my professional thoughts. Can we have lunch?"

"I've already eaten lunch."

41

"Not today. Saturday perhaps. Name the restaurant."

I wanted to name a restaurant in Hong Kong and let him show up and I wouldn't. He was really into this adoption thing. He was after my mind.

"Dr. Slime . . ." I said.

"The name's Wasserman. . . ."

"Sorry. This is a very busy week for me. I've got a lot of matters to take care of."

"Next week, then."

"Next week is shaping up busy, too."

"Next month?"

"Maybe you could just tell me over the telephone."

"No, it's better to talk on a full, happy stomach."

"Okay. I'll get a sandwich and some munchies from the refrigerator and you get a sandwich and some munchies and we'll bring them back to the telephone and we'll eat and talk."

"No, no, no. It's not the same as having lunch in a nice restaurant. I think you're trying to avoid me." Dr. Wasserman laughed.

Chapter 8

I get a lot of ideas at night. It may have something to do with where the moon is at in relation to where my head is at, but I'm not sure about that.

Anyway, I got a midnight idea about Jack and Lee and the next day I went out and put it into action. I bought two tickets to *Monster Mayhem* and what I figured was two hours' worth of jelly beans. I had been saving my money to buy more records, but what's a friend for if he can't go broke for his two best pals.

I put one ticket and half of the jelly beans in a jar, and the other ticket and the other half of the jelly beans in another jar. That was the easy part of my plan. The hard part was to put the two jars in the right places without being seen.

I went to the locker room at school and waited until there were so many kids around that nobody paid any attention to me. But I made sure that none of the kids were Jack or Lee. Then I put one jar in Jack's locker and the other jar in Lee's locker. I know their combinations. I also left a note in Jack's locker: *From your forever friend, Lee.* I left a note in Lee's locker: *From your forever friend, Jack.*

It was so simple. Jack would think that Lee had given him half of the prize. And Lee would think that Jack had given him half of the prize. They would instantly make up. This was definitely one of my best plans ever, and I stationed myself in the locker room to watch the great event take place.

Lee's and Jack's lockers are about twelve lockers apart. My locker is between them. I waited for Jack and Lee to show up. I pretended to be busy opening my locker, taking things out, putting things in, dropping things, picking them up, counting them, and counting them again. Would they *never* come? At last they did. They came separately, of course, but at about the same time.

I watched them. I saw Lee open his locker, take out some books, and then the jar and the note. He looked surprised. I watched him read the note. Then I saw him reach inside the jar, take out a jelly bean, and eat it very slowly. I figured he was either testing for poison or accepting the gift, since he was using it. So far, so good.

I turned and looked at Jack. He was putting things in his locker. Then I saw him find the note, take it out, and read it. Then he took out the jar and held it up to the light. He might have been checking for scorpions. I'll never know.

I turned back to see what Lee was doing. He was

44

walking over to Jack. He had to pass me to do it. I stuck my head inside my locker as if I had urgent business there. Then I withdrew quickly so I could watch this perfect meeting between Jack and Lee, this wonderful making-up moment brought to them through the clever thinking of their great pal Frank.

Lee said to Jack, "Thanks for giving me this stuff, Jack."

"What stuff?" asked Jack.

At that hideous instant I knew there was a big hole in my strategy. But it was too late.

"This stuff," said Lee. He held up his jar like it was a trophy. "All these jelly beans and the ticket to *Monster Mayhem*. You gave up your share of the prize for me. To show that you know I'm right and you're wrong."

"What? *You're* right and *I'm* wrong?"

"You've got it," said Lee.

Jack looked inside his jar. "I'll tell you what I've got," he said. "I've got a ticket to *Monster Mayhem* and enough jelly beans to feed ten gorillas."

"Where did you get that?" asked Lee.

"From you."

"From *me*?"

"Sure. Are you playing dumb. Here's your card." Jack held up his From Your Forever Friend Lee card.

And while I started to creep out of sight, Lee held up his From Your Forever Friend Jack card.

Jack and Lee were madder than ever.

"Is this your idea of a joke?" Lee asked Jack.

"How could it be my idea of a joke when I got the same stuff you got? *Think!*"

"I can think without your telling me to!"

45

They both yelled, "Frank!"

I could hear them but I couldn't see them. I, Frank, had already left the locker room. With a new philosophy of life. Never pull anything on guys who are planning to use their heads as a career. Limit yourself to those kids who are counting on their bodies or looks or luck to get them by. Those types might not have caught on to a plan that was too dumb to have been thought up by a smart kid like me.

Jack and Lee were too mad at each other to be mad at me. I could go on forever doing these things and they wouldn't get mad at *me*.

That's what I was counting on when I made up my mind that I would keep trying. Only the next time there would be no tricky scheme. Just a good, basic idea that only a genius could think up.

Chapter 9

I was now walking to and from school with Jack *or* Lee. Never the three of us together. I *had* to do something about that. But what? I was waiting, waiting . . .

Sometimes, on the way to school Lee stops in a bank. It's boring, but I tag along. One morning before school we were passing the bank across the street from the Merry Midtown Mall.

"Let's go in and look at the withdrawal and deposit slips," said Lee. "They change the style from time to time. We have to keep up with these things."

"We do?"

We went inside. I waited while Lee looked over all the slips. Then he just stood there and watched the customers.

"Let's leave," I said.

"You can learn a lot about the banking business by

watching customers," said Lee. "Especially their feet. See those people standing in line? The ones with the scroungy shoes want to borrow money. The ones with the polished shoes are going to make a deposit. Sneakers? It's hard to tell about sneakers. There are dirty poor sneakers and dirty rich sneakers. Next you look at skin tones. The people with tans have come back from vacation. They were rich enough to take a vacation, so they probably have money to deposit. Unless the vacation wiped them out. The pale people are like sneakers. You just can't tell about them."

"We'll be late for school, Lee."

"There could be a holdup person in line, too. Statistically, one out of every thousand people who go into a bank is a robber. That's my own statistic."

"The bank guard is looking at us suspiciously," I said.

"Good. That means he's doing his job. The uniform makes him sure of himself. At home his wife probably picks on him and makes him take out the garbage."

"Here comes Bianca Wasserman and her mother," I said.

"Nice try, Frank. But I'm not leaving yet. I—you're right! It's *them*!"

Lee ran out of the bank. The guard started to go after him, then shrugged and stopped. Bianca and half of The Couple Who Ate Cleveland advanced on me.

Bianca's mother said, "I know you. You were the werewolf, weren't you? I never forget a face."

I was relieved to be remembered just as a werewolf. Bianca's mother didn't seem to be in on her husband's adoption plan.

Bianca said, "Was that Lee running out of here? He's never home when I call him."

Bianca's mother frowned. "Does his mother know he's out on the streets so much? I'd be worried sick if I didn't know where my Bianca was. Her volunteer work on the phone keeps her so busy."

"Volunteer work?"

"Yes, all those phone calls to cheer up shut-ins."

"Shut-ins? But she doesn't make calls to—"

Bianca froze me with a look.

"I'm taking Bianca to school right after I make this deposit. Would you like a ride?"

No, I wouldn't like a ride with Bianca and her mother, but I knew that Lee would be long gone and I'd be late for school without a ride.

"Thanks," I said.

While Bianca's mother made her deposit, Bianca whispered, "Look, maybe I make a *few* phony phone calls but I don't do all the weird things *you* do. So clam up."

Bianca didn't speak to me on the ride to school in the Wasserman Cadillac. She was probably afraid I'd say something about her phony phone calls. She was afraid of her mother.

At school I was seen getting out of a car with Bianca Wasserman. It was not going to be a good day for me. I had spent part of it in a bank, part of it with Bianca Wasserman and her mother, and it was still early in the morning.

But I was getting a new idea. I always carry out my ideas by myself. Frank Kalpal doesn't need help. Yet help was getting out of the Wasserman Cadillac with me. Bianca tried to walk ahead of me into school.

50

"Bianca, stop!"

Bianca turned around. "Well?"

"Let's talk."

"About what?"

"Phony phone calls. You mean your mother doesn't *know*?"

"Of course not," said Bianca. "She and my father have all these theories about aggression and hostility. So I'm allowed to walk on sofas. Great! Who wants to walk on a sofa? But if she knew about the phone calls, she'd tie it in with hostility or something. Who knows what she'd do about it. So I keep this list with the names of nursing homes and hospitals by the phone, and she thinks I call them. You won't tell, will you?"

"No, but you could do me a little favor."

"That sounds like a bribe," said Bianca. "I mean 'no' and 'but you could do me a little favor' coming so close together."

"Just think of it as a favor to both of us," I said.

"Both of us?"

"Yeah. See, Bianca, you're not very good at what you do. No offense, but everyone recognizes your voice. And your excuses for calling are—well, they're not funny. Phony phone calls are a very special art form. They should either be really funny or else they should be realistic. They should fool somebody completely. A dognapping service really doesn't do it. Not funny and not fooling anybody."

Bianca was angry. "It isn't nice to tell someone they're not good at what they do best. I could be psychologically scarred for life just by hearing you say what you just said."

51

"No, there's hope. I can give you a chance to make a *real* call and fool somebody. I'll give you that opportunity."

"Opportunity is the favorite word of con artists, Frank."

After all these years in school, I was just now getting to know Bianca Wasserman. Her teeth always seemed like an obstacle to getting to know her head. I can't explain that except that they were like two big blanks advertising that more blanks were to be found inside. But now I was thinking that she was pretty smart. She probably picked up a lot of knowledge from her parents when they weren't busy being crazy.

"All you'd have to do is make one telephone call to a radio station and say that you're either Jack Redtress's mother or Lee Goodfellow's mother. You have your choice of mothers. Then you say that the boys aren't allowed to eat jelly beans or attend monster movies. So they're both forfeiting the contest prize. All you have to do is say those words. And sound older. Like somebody's mother."

Bianca giggled. "I'll do it."

All during the school day I felt pretty good. I now had a partner. And a new plan. I knew that the contest prize hadn't been given out yet. By the time Station KNIF found out that Jack and Lee hadn't forfeited the prize, the person who guessed the next nearest number of jelly beans would have eaten them and seen the movie. The contest would be dead.

After school Bianca and I went to her house. It was still a mess from the party. We went up to the telephone in her room. Beside the phone was a long piece

of paper with a list that started with Happy Haven Retirement Village.

I looked up the telephone number of Station KNIF. "Ask for the manager or somebody in charge," I said. "Now repeat to me what you're going to say."

"I remember," said Bianca. "I'm supposed to be either Jack Redtress's mother or Lee Goodfellow's mother and the boys aren't allowed to eat jelly beans or attend monster movies so they're forfeiting the contest prize. See? I've got a super memory."

Bianca dialed the number of the radio station. "May I speak to the manager or somebody in charge, please?"

She was wonderful! Her voice sounded almost middle-aged. Bianca had real talent on the telephone. I'd have to compliment her after the call.

There was a pause. Then Bianca spoke again. "Hello, Mister Manager?" she said. "This is either Jack Redtress's mother or Lee Goodfellow's mother."

As my fingers pressed the button to cut off the call, I realized that Bianca was not as smart as I thought she was. I should have believed her teeth.

I also knew that Frank Kalpal, for better or for worse, would always work alone.

Chapter 10

I am not the only schemer in the world. There was a
master brain at work at Station KNIF. Two master
brains. They belonged to Tasha and Daddy-O, the two
people who ran the station. Their brains were not what
you would call high quality or anything like that. Otherwise they would not have dreamed up their fiendish
plan to have Jack and Lee each eat their one hour's
worth of jelly beans in the middle of the mall.

Jack and Lee went along with it. It was a chance to
win! Some win. There are not too many things more
disgusting than watching two boys eat a high percentage of the world's supply of jelly beans. Maybe eating a
live octopus or something of that nature. I hoped there
would be an ambulance standing by. Can you pump
out a stomach full of jelly beans?

Jack and Lee were seated on a platform in the mall

next to jars and jars and jars and jars and jars and jars of jelly beans. They didn't speak to each other. There was a bunch of kids from school and a crowd of people in the mall watching and whispering.

Tasha and Daddy-O strode out onto the platform. They waited for applause from the crowd. They looked like the kind of couple who would think up a demented plan like this. They both had bright-red hair and were loaded down with pins that said KNIF Knows Kids. Tasha had some fur stuff slung around her neck, and unfortunately there was what looked like the head of a dead fox attached to it. It was revolting. Daddy-O was wearing a gold sailor suit. Both of them were dressed as if they had bought their clothes from a Halloween catalogue.

Tasha walked up to the microphone. A spotlight beamed down on her. It lighted up the dead fox's face. It was revolting all over again. Some of the kids said, *"Yecchh!"* I hoped it would spoil Jack's and Lee's appetites.

"Welcome to the Jelly Bean Marathon," said Tasha. "And now, here we go! Ready, set, eat!"

Jack and Lee each grabbed a jar and started to eat the jelly beans. They ate and ate. Empty jars collected around their feet.

How could I stop them! There must be a law against something like this. Why hadn't I looked it up! Maybe they didn't tell their parents. *I* could tell their parents. But it would be too late to stop this Challenge of the Gluttons. I had to do something quick and dramatic.

Sudden death! That was it. There is nothing more attention-getting than sudden death.

I took a deep breath. Then I yelled as loud as I could, "EEEeeeeee!!" and keeled over.

There was a problem. The crowd was so noisy, no one heard me. And the crowd was so big that no matter how hard I keeled, I ended up simply leaning on some people next to me.

"Can't you stand up straight!" one of them said.

Lemon Derringer was looking at me. "Are you pretending to die again, Frank? I'm so bored with that one."

Jack and Lee kept on eating. But they were eating a little slower. And looking a little sick.

I needed something that would get more attention than sudden death. I looked around. I saw a shoe store, a bookstore, a clothing store, and a pet store. A pet store! Animals always get more attention than people. Maybe I could get a snake or something and release it into the crowd.

I pushed my way out of the crowd and ran to the pet store. A man was standing just inside. He was holding a kitten. "I need a snake or a mouse or something equally repulsive," I said.

The man looked at me suspiciously. "Most people want cute pets," he said. "You have something particularly repulsive in mind?"

I reached into my pocket. "I've got three dollars. What can you sell me fast for three dollars?"

The man waved his hand around the store. "I have a trained ant, a few goldfish, and plenty of gerbils."

"How about a nonpoisonous snake?"

"Nothing under ten bucks."

"A mouse?"

"A mouse? We don't get any requests for mice. There's too much competition from private households. Want a mouse? Look in your house. But if you're interested in a rodent, we have plenty of gerbils. They're on special this week. Most kids think they're cute. Oh, I forgot. You don't want cute. You want repulsive."

"Gerbils are fast, aren't they?"

"You'd better believe it."

"I'll take one."

"Which one?"

"The fastest."

The man got a gerbil and put it into a box with holes in the lid. I paid him the money and ran out of the store.

"Wait!" he called. "Don't you want to know how to take care of it? Don't you want to know its name? You're carrying Mildred, and she needs tender loving care!"

There was a bigger crowd than before. I ran to the edge of it. Lemon Derringer was watching me! She must have watched me go into the pet store. But I couldn't stop now.

I bent down and opened the box. After that, it all happened so fast I couldn't believe it. Mildred ran out. Lemon screamed, "A mouse! A rat! It touched me! It touched me! I'm contaminated!"

The crowd started to fall apart as if a wind had come along and blown it. I couldn't see Mildred but I could tell where she was because that's where the screams were coming from. On the stage Jack and Lee stopped eating. Tasha and Daddy-O looked mad.

Mildred ran up onto the platform. It was easy. The

58

crowd had cleared the way for her. She knocked over a couple of jars of jelly beans.

Suddenly Tasha reached down and scooped up Mildred. "Gotcha, you little rodent," she said. She spoke to the crowd. "It's only a gerbil. Now will its owner please claim it so we can get on with the contest."

I was standing with my open gerbil box. Lemon pointed to me. "*He* did it. He's been doing nutsies like that for years. Ever since kindergarten. He did it, he did it, he did it! I'm contaminated."

Lemon ran off. People were looking at me. Then more people. It caught on. I was the center of attention. "Oh, I guess my gerbil got loose," I said. "Thanks for catching it."

I walked up the platform. Jack and Lee were smiling at me. They were glad about the gerbil! I had saved them from about ten minutes of jelly beans. Now if I could only get them to smile at each other.

Tasha was talking to the crowd. "We will extend the contest for another ten minutes beyond the hour to make up for the time we lost."

She was sadistic, that's what she was.

I walked over to her and held up my box so that she could put Mildred into it. As she bent down, the dead fox's face on the end of her fur thing brushed against my face. "*Yecchh!*" I said. As I pushed the fur thing away from me, I tipped the box. Mildred escaped as the fur thing unwound from Tasha's neck and fell to the ground. I was so used to doing stuff on purpose that I couldn't believe all this was happening without my even trying.

Mildred ran into the crowd again. The fur thing lay on the ground. Tasha seemed stupefied.

I looked down at the fur piece. I thought about the fox and how it must have run through the woods and leaped and breathed when it was alive. It wouldn't have wanted to end up around somebody's fat neck.

Foxes aren't my specialty, but I never say no to opportunity. I reached down, picked up the fur piece, and threw it high into the air. I watched it sail over the crowd. The fox almost seemed alive, beautiful, a graceful creature on the move.

There was now a furry creature on the ground and a furry creature in the air. Everyone ducked and screamed. Then they ran like crazy. It was a bigger retreat than I have ever seen in a battle scene in a movie.

The contest was over, no doubt about that.

Chapter 11

The morning after the jelly bean–eating competition, Jack and Lee met me on the way to school. They were laughing. They were *together*!

"What are you doing together?" I asked.

"Hey, is there a law against it?" Jack asked.

"Well, you were going kind of hot and heavy over the jelly bean stuff."

"It's over," said Lee. "Didn't you notice that, yesterday in the mall? When that lady's fox took off?"

"And the gerbil," said Jack.

Now the three of us were laughing.

"You did okay, Frank," said Jack, and he gave me a friendly nudge.

"It was beautiful," said Lee.

"The Sticky Three's beautiful," I said. I had this sudden wish that somebody would come up and snap,

snap, take a picture of the three of us together. I wanted to think that *I* had brought this fantastic moment about, that this reunion between Jack and Lee was made possible by me, Perfectly Frank. But I couldn't take all the credit for it. Tasha and Daddy-O had thought up the fiendish jelly bean–eating plan. How could such a rotten plan turn out so well?

It didn't turn out completely well. During the next few days I found out that Tasha and Daddy-O were looking for the "Rodent Releaser." That was Tasha's name for me. Jack and Lee weren't going to tell on me. Neither were the other kids from school who had been in the mall. Including Lemon Derringer. "I report to the principal," she said, "not to a dead-fox lady or a gold sailor." But I didn't feel safe walking in the mall. The pet store owner had described me as "the boy with the ferret eyes."

At the end of the week, things got worse. The principal, Mr. Sklish, wanted to see me.

The principal of our school is a person to avoid. He's one of those people who cleans his teeth about ten times a day (he carries a toothbrush in his pocket), and he stands erect and does everything by the rules. He makes up the rules and I guess that's why he does everything by them. If he didn't have his rules, he would have nothing to uphold and be firm about and drive the kids nuts over.

Mr. Sklish has been after me ever since I entered Nathan Clifford Elementary School. He had heard rumors about me that were left over from kindergarten. But he could never prove anything. Would today be my downfall? Had Lemon Derringer produced her *proof*?

I walked into Mr. Sklish's office, and I hoped I wasn't cringing.

"Hi, Mr. Sklish."

He gave me a stony stare. "Your attempt to be friendly only makes me more suspicious of you, Frank."

"You're suspicious of me?"

"Highly." Mr. Sklish circled around me. "There's something about you . . ."

"A halo maybe?"

"A rumor. Many rumors. Ever since I heard that very first one—the one about your painting a toilet green and orange in the boys' lavatory—I've been suspicious of you." Mr. Sklish sighed. "That was followed by the rumor that you painted a sink to match in the girls' lavatory."

"Now how could I have gotten in there?"

"Only you know that," said Mr. Sklish. "For four years now I've been out to get you. You're what I would call a holy crusade. I am going to *catch you in the act.*"

"What act?"

"*Any* act. It was my misfortune that I wasn't at the mall the other day. If I had been, I'd have caught you when you released that gerbil and sent a dead fox flying through the air. Lemon Derringer told me all about it. She said she brought me *proof!*"

Mr. Sklish held up a piece of fur. "She claims that this bit of fur is from the gerbil you released into the crowd. Do you own a gerbil?"

"No."

"Did you ever own a gerbil?"

"Briefly, very briefly, I owned a gerbil named Mildred. But she, uh, got away from me."

Mr. Sklish put the fur down. "This fur could belong to *any* gerbil. So it's not proof. Sadly I have to add it to my ever growing collection of items that Lemon has brought me over the years. Someday she'll strike it right."

Mr. Sklish carefully put a label around the piece of fur, and then placed the fur in a desk drawer. He labeled it Exhibit 43.

"I don't understand why an honor student like you gets involved in these dreary escapades, Frank. I believe you need an outlet for all your energy. So I have a suggestion. Take up a hobby, Frank. A good worthwhile hobby. Like collecting paper clips."

"Paper clips?"

"Yes. Nobody respects them and that's why they're disappearing from the world, as surely as the dinosaurs did. Extinction is just around the corner for paper clips, Frank. Now if you put your energies into something *constructive* instead of *destructive*, I'm sure I won't be hearing any more rumors about you."

"You want me to collect paper clips? That's what you said?"

"Exactly. When you have one thousand, report back to me."

"Where do I find them?"

"On floors, in wastebaskets, wherever careless people have dropped or tossed them."

"Okay."

"You agree?"

"Sure. I'll be back in one thousand paper clips."

"Just a moment," said Mr. Sklish.

He dropped a paper clip on the floor. Then he picked it up and handed it to me. "Here," he said. "To get you started and inspire you."

"Thanks," I said.

"Remember, don't come back until you reach your quota."

"I won't," I said.

I walked out of Mr. Sklish's office. I flipped the paper clip into the air. If I were really fast about it and looked really hard, it probably wouldn't take me more than a hundred years to collect a thousand paper clips.

I was in a good mood. Mr. Sklish wouldn't be bugging me for a long time. Lemon Derringer had failed again. Yahoo!

Chapter 12

My day wasn't over. There was more. And here it was:
Bianca Wasserman had a crush on me. This is how I
knew. She came up to me in the middle of the auditorium at school and said, "Kiss me, Frank."

I said, *"What?"*

"You heard me. Kiss me, Frank. Here. Now."

"Why?"

"Because I want you to."

"Girls don't ask boys to kiss them," I said.

"Well, they *should*. That's what my mother and father
say. They say it's a healthy thing to do. I cleared this
with them before I asked you to kiss me. They said,
'Full speed ahead,' that's what they said."

"You asked *their* permission to ask *me* to kiss *you*? Do
I have that sequence right?"

"You do."

"I thought you, uh, liked Jack and Lee."

"I did. But that was then and this is now and I like you."

"I don't kiss people in auditoriums. I wouldn't kiss my mother in an auditorium."

"Then how about after school in my garage with the doors closed?"

"Bianca, let's talk about this next week. By next week you might want to kiss an entirely different person, and you'll be sorry that you asked me to kiss you. The memory of my kissing you would definitely spoil it for you next week. So think ahead, okay?"

"Not okay."

I started to walk away. But Bianca called after me, "Remember when I was either Jack Redtress's mother or Lee Goodfellow's mother?"

"Shh!" I rushed back to Bianca. She certainly knew the right mating call. "Bianca," I said, "I remember that as clearly as I remember your *phony phone calls.* Get it?"

"I gave them up. I threw away my list of nursing homes and hospitals."

"Why would you give up those phony phone calls when they meant so much to you?"

"They represented a psychological phase in my development that's temporary. I read it in one of my parents' books. There's a time to make phony phone calls and a time to stop, and now I've stopped. But you're never going to stop what you do, are you?"

"What *do* I do, Bianca?" I wondered how much she knew.

"Well, actually I don't know what you do, except it

68

seems to be devious. And am I ever attracted to *devious*. Kiss me, Frank."

"Bianca, you should stop talking to your parents."

"How can I do that? They're the only other people in the house."

"Tell them you don't need their advice. Tell them they're too old for you. Then get yourself a wonderful, wonderful friend your own age who has common sense."

"You mean like you, Frank?"

"Well."

"I'd like to be your friend, Frank. Like, you know, a sincere and true friend. I'll forget the kiss. Let's just be friends."

Bianca was staring at me, almost pleading, and there I was, her only alternative to her wacko parents. She was offering me sincere and true friendship. I had no idea what that meant, coming from her.

"Does this have anything to do with entering your garage?" I asked.

"No, it's about wanting the good feeling that somebody likes you and cares about you. That's all."

Poor Bianca. She got so many theories from her parents that she had probably been drowning in them. And now she had suddenly figured out for herself what she really wanted. A friend. Me.

"Okay, we're friends," I said. I almost leaned over and gave her a little kiss on the cheek. Almost.

I walked away. Then I turned around. Bianca was still standing there. She raised her hand and gave a little wave. Then she smiled a little smile. She seemed shy. Would this new Bianca ever again give one of her nutty parties? Would she ever try to communicate again via her phony phone calls? Or was she at last on the right track? I couldn't tell her that you can't really be friends with someone just by *saying* you are. But it's a good start. And somehow, in just a few minutes in the middle of the auditorium, I had done more for friendship than in all my schemes to get Jack and Lee back together again.

Chapter 13

My life was perfect. Jack, Lee, and I were closer than ever. Lemon Derringer had quieted down. Ms. Pillsbury forgot to call me a genius, and Mr. Sklish simply gave me a paper clip salute whenever he saw me.

But Bianca was having another party. She called Jack and Lee and me and invited us in a normal way. She told us that we were even allowed to come as normal people. What was going on? I remembered her last party and how I got myself an adoptive father. Once you've been adopted by green slime, it sticks with you. It makes you wonder about yourself and how things happen to you that don't happen to average kids. Most of all, it makes your mind want to go and take a shower.

Jack, Lee, and I went to the party together, of course. It felt so great being part of The Sticky Three again.

Jack and Lee were back to competing on paper for millions and millions of dollars. All very harmless. But we were at the Wassermans' door, so how long could the great feeling last? I was pretty sure we'd be greeted by Mr. and Mrs. Slime Who Ate Cleveland.

Blitz Melnick answered the door. This was the first time I'd ever seen him at one of Bianca's parties.

"The Sticky Three!" he said. "Two jelly beans and a genius."

The three of us reached out to grab Blitz. But Bianca and her mother rushed up. "No aggression allowed!" said Bianca. "This is a new kind of party."

"Indeed!" said her mother. Bianca's mother was dressed like an ordinary person. It was true, the Wassermans were into normalcy. I was sure when her father came up looking as clean and bland as Mr. Sklish.

"Hello, boys," he said.

Boys! He didn't single me out as *son*. Did he even remember me? He kept talking. "This is Bianca's birthday, and we're starting a new era. She and her friends— all of you—are on your way to maturity. No more running around here."

"You mean that Bianca's parties aren't going to be fun anymore?" asked a girl who was standing in back of Bianca. "We can't walk on tables?"

"No more tables," said Bianca's mother.

"I wish I had known it was Bianca's birthday," I said. "I would have brought a present. The three of us would have—right, guys?"

Jack and Lee nodded.

"Don't be concerned, son," said Dr. Wasserman. "Loners like you tend to overthink."

Son. Loner. He remembered.

"I'm not a loner," I said. "You can see I'm not alone. Jack and Lee and I, we're best friends. We're together all the time. We're The Sticky Three."

"Forever," said Jack.

"You bet," said Lee.

Jack and Lee were on my side all the way. It was nice. It was the three of us vs. Dr. Wasserman. I figured we won. The adoption was a lost cause.

Not quite.

"You mean the three of you hang around together all the time?" Dr. Wasserman scratched his head. "There's never a fourth person? Or a fifth? How about a girl? You need a girl in your little group."

I knew what girl he had in mind. She was staring at us hopefully.

Jack and Lee looked at me. I was supposed to get us out of this before it went any further. I was supposed to match wits and weirdness with Dr. Wasserman and come out on top. They had much too much faith in me.

I tried to get the subject back to birthday presents. I said, "Jack, Lee, and I really want to get you a nice present for your birthday, Bianca."

"No, no, no!" Dr. Wasserman said before Bianca could say anything. "No presents. But we're all going to make cards for Bianca right here at the party. Bianca prefers that to receiving something commercial and plastic purchased at a store."

Bianca didn't look so sure about that. She certainly loved her commercial plastic telephone.

"I'd rather eat than make cards," said Lemon Derringer.

Lemon Derringer! What was *she* doing here? Bianca had never invited *her* to a party before. I looked around. The room was filled with kids. This must be a new plan for Bianca's life. Collecting friends, like stamps or coins. Or paper clips.

But Bianca was acting like she liked it, so maybe she did. Having a birthday makes you feel important, and having a crowd to share it with makes you feel even more important. This must have been the strategy of Doctors Glinka and Max Wasserman.

I waited to see what would happen next. I hoped something would happen. I didn't want Bianca's father to get back to his new plan to expand The Sticky Three to The Sticky Four or Five.

"Everybody please sit down," said Bianca, like she was the boss. Which she was.

Everybody sat down on the floor. Bianca and her parents handed out colored paper and sparkles and paste and crayons and everything a well-equipped kindergarten should have.

Lemon started to shake a bottle of paste.

Bianca's mother kind of made a face, but she didn't say anything.

"Young lady," said Bianca's father, "be careful of that paste. This carpeting cost thousands of dollars."

Suddenly Bianca's parents were concerned about messes. It hit me what was happening. It wasn't Bianca who was growing up, it was *them*. They were getting

74

fussy and picky and careful just the way parents are supposed to be.

"I'll go get some newspapers to put under everything," Bianca's mother said. She left the room and returned with a big pile of newspapers. She handed some to everybody.

"Time to catch up on my reading," said Blitz. He pretended to turn pages. "What's news?"

"Stop fooling around, Blitz," said Bianca.

Blitz didn't pay any attention to her. "Hey, what's this?" he said. "A chance to win a hundred dollars. The newspaper's having a contest."

Contest? I didn't want to hear that word. That word was part of my past.

"Make your card, Blitz," I said.

But Blitz was waving the newspaper. "Who wants to win one hundred dollars? All you have to do is finish the sentence *I read* The Arizona Daily Times *because* in twenty-five words or less."

Lemon grabbed the newspaper. "They pay you one hundred dollars for writing twenty-five words or less? In school they don't pay anything."

"Twenty-five words or less?" said Jack. "That could be like four dollars a word."

"I already figured that out," said Lee.

"Hey, it's another contest for you two to enter," said Bianca.

It was time for me to speak up, to put an end to all of this. "It's not a contest for Jack and Lee," I said, "because it isn't their kind of contest. It's just words, not figures or anything."

"I'm good at words," said Jack.

75

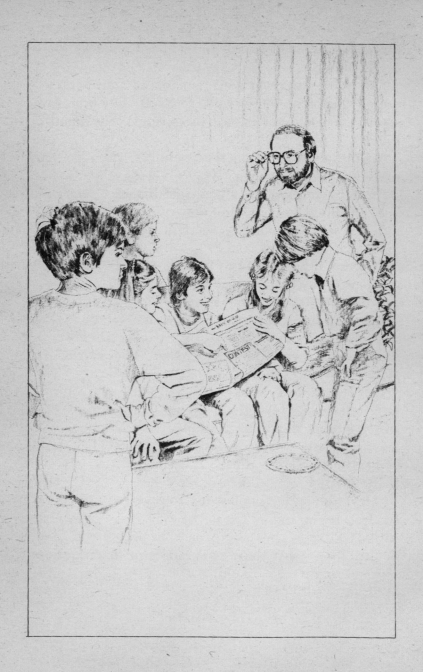

"So am I," said Lee. "I can think of a lot of four-dollar words."

"I can think of eight-dollar words," said Jack.

I could see the jelly beans rising from their grave and turning into words. "Let's make cards for Bianca," I said.

"I don't want cards," said Bianca. "This is more fun. It's better than jelly beans. Jack or Lee could get rich."

"Who says they're entering this contest?" I asked, hoping for silence.

"I do," said Jack.

"Me too," said Lee.

Bianca's father spoke up. "I don't want to discourage you boys, but this contest is really for adults."

Blitz grabbed the newspaper back from Lemon. "It doesn't say that here. It only says something about you can't enter if you're a relative of the newspaper."

"No, that's not what I mean," said Bianca's father. "I'm saying that adults have more sophisticated ideas. You boys can't hope to compete against that."

I was changing my mind about Bianca's father. Not that I ever wanted to be his son, but at that moment I felt like saying, "You tell 'em, Pops." Then I remembered his green face and his green body from the last party.

I said simply, "Dr. Wasserman is right. The newspaper's making a big mistake, pitting children against adults."

"Children?" said Jack. "I'm not a child. Eat those words, Frank."

"I'm not hungry," I said.

Chapter 14

I face facts, no matter what. That's why I call myself Perfectly Frank. And I had a fact to face. Jack and Lee were about to get into another fight over another contest. It was my job to prevent that. Back to work!

I called the newspaper before I could change my mind.

"The Arizona Daily Times," a voice answered.

"I'd like to speak to whoever is in charge of your Twenty-five Words or Less contest."

"One moment."

The moment took forever. Then a man's voice said, "Aristotle Albert here."

"Are you the contest person?"

"I'm a reporter."

"I need to talk to your contest person."

"Is there a problem?"

"You better believe it. That Twenty-five Words or Less contest that your newspaper is running. It discriminates against children. I happen to know that your paper is very big on discrimination issues, and now you're causing one."

"I don't understand."

"Well, who do you think is going to win that contest? An adult. Someone who's been reading newspapers for years and years. A kid doesn't have a chance."

"Young man, are you looking for a cause? If so, this isn't a very good one. Why don't you take on, say, school cafeterias? I ate in one once. Now *there's* a case of blatant discrimination against children."

"Don't change the subject. You should drop this contest immediately. Contests can be lethal. I know of one that almost wrecked a friendship between two boys. A jelly bean–counting contest."

"But kids are always fighting."

"Don't say *but*. The world is a cold place when you don't have a friend that you once had."

"You have a point," said Mr. Albert. I thought I heard him sigh.

Then he asked. "How old are you? What's your name?"

"I know why you're asking. You're thinking, a cute story about kids. A kitchy-koo story. An adorable story, right?"

He hadn't said anything about a story. What was happening to me? I was beginning to feel important. I could make things happen. I had a place in the world. I had the ear of a newspaper reporter. This was no time to withhold facts.

I spoke up. "My name is Frank Kalpal and I'm eleven."

There was a pause. Then Mr. Albert asked, "Do I know you? Your name sounds familiar. Wait a minute. Are you the kid who tried to import a camel into Arizona last year?"

"I might be."

"Someone telephoned the newspaper about it, but we thought it was just a rumor. Now I'm not so sure."

"Uh, my parents don't know about that one, so could you just forget it please. But about my friends—"

"You sound like an interesting kid. Gutsy. Hold on a minute. I'm connecting you with 'Youth of the Month.' "

"Huh?"

"Natasha, this one's for you," I heard Mr. Albert say. Then I couldn't hear anything. Mr. Albert and Natasha must be having a private conversation. About me? Maybe I should hang up. Getting switched around from person to person makes you feel like somebody's trying to get rid of you by passing you on.

At last I heard something.

"Hi, Frank. This is Natasha Harry. I'd like to come over and talk with you. Would three o'clock tomorrow afternoon be convenient? I suppose you're out of school by then."

I said, "Do you mean you're going to *interview* me? Like with a tape recorder?"

"I use a notebook. And yes, I'd like to interview you. A photographer will also be over. I don't know exactly when. It depends on his other assignments."

Assignments. Photographer. Notebook. Interview. All wonderful words.

After the conversation was over, I was so excited I

almost forgot about Jack and Lee. This interview might make me a little famous, and I had to think about *that*.

I hoped the reporter would spell my name right. Should I tell her how to remember it?

K as in kangaroo
A as in ant
L as in liverwurst
P as in plant
A as in ant again
L as in plant again
if you leave off the p
Which you should!
The pea is a shriveled green thing
on your plate
that you're always terribly
sorry you ate.

Maybe the reporter was a good speller without any help.

Chapter 15

I had to tell my mother and father that a newspaper reporter was coming the next day. My parents love me, but they worry a lot. Mostly about me.

I waited until we were all sitting down at dinner and my father asked, "How was your day, Frank?"

He always asks that.

"Interesting."

"Interesting? It's a new one, isn't it, Frank?"

"A new what?"

"You know what. Your mother and I would prefer that you don't have interesting days. We like quiet days, peaceful days, boring days. Remember the last interesting day you had, Frank? The sheriff came by."

"He was selling raffles."

"No matter. I think it's illegal for sheriffs to sell

raffles. I can smell a ruse a mile away. He was sniffing us out."

My mother spoke up. "I have just a few simple questions. Frank, whatever you're doing now, will it cause the electric company to cut off our service again? Remember the neon lights you put up on the front porch to announce the birth of your pet toad?"

"A reporter's coming over. That's all."

My father looked at me. "An investigative reporter?"

"No. A plain reporter."

My father shrugged at me. "Why not."

"Why not," said my mother.

I went to my room to pick out what I was going to wear for my picture. I chose my striped shirt that makes me look like a real athlete. That would be a good angle for the newspaper story too. Reporters like it when you're versatile, when you don't do just one thing like trying to bring friends together again.

The next day in school I kept quiet about the interview. As soon as school was over I ran right home. First thing, I changed my shirt. I looked in the mirror. My hair looked peculiar. Hair almost always looks peculiar at the exact time you especially don't want it to. All other times it looks fine.

My father was at work. My mother is an artist and she works at home. She said she was going to stay in her studio and keep out of my way, that it was "my show."

Natasha Harry was ten minutes late. She shook hands with me when she arrived. I'm not sure if she looked like a reporter because I had never seen one before. But she sized me up as if she was already starting to write about me in her head.

After we said hi and hello and that kind of stuff, she sat down on the couch and took out her pad and pencil. I sat down in a chair across from her. I started to talk before she could ask any questions. First I told her I didn't want to discuss camels. Then I started to talk about The Sticky Three. I hoped it sounded colorful for the newspaper. I told her all about the jelly bean contest and how it had messed up Jack and Lee's friendship. And how much I wanted Jack and Lee to be friends forever. When I ran down, Natasha started to ask questions. She kept calling me Frank, like I was an old buddy of hers. Most of her questions were about me, just me. About my hobbies, and school, and my future plans. I told her lots, including that I think modesty is dishonest. I think she smiled at that, but I can't be sure.

Then she closed her pad and put away her pencil. She got up to leave. She said the photographer would be along soon. Before I could ask, she said the article would be in next Sunday's paper.

"It's been an honor meeting you, Frank."

An honor! Better than a pleasure, or whatever grown-ups say.

My mother came out to say hello and good-bye to Natasha. I stood at a distance while they talked. I heard Natasha say "enterprising kid" to my mother. I could tell she thought I was headed for Harvard.

Then she said good-bye to both of us and was out the door. I looked at the kitchen clock. The interview had only taken twenty minutes. Reporters are fast.

The photographer showed up just a few minutes after Natasha left. He had lots of stuff slung over his shoulder, like he was on a safari. He was fast too. He checked the lighting in different rooms, opened drapes, and generally made himself at home. Then he took a bunch of pictures of me in my room, which I had forgotten to clean. But he seemed to like it messy, as if he had found the perfect setting for me. He asked if I had a dog and I said no. But his eyes lit up when he saw my cat in the laundry room. He took three shots with me holding my cat. He kept saying "Good" and "Great" after every shot.

"How come you're taking so many pictures?" I asked politely. I wondered if there would be a whole spread of them in the newspaper.

"It gives us a good selection to choose from," he said as he packed up his equipment and almost rushed out the door. Newspaper people are sure in a hurry.

He said, "Nice cat," as he left.

Chapter 16

Sunday morning I was the first on my block to get the newspaper. I was outside in the cold, shivering in the dark, waiting for it.

My hands were shaking when I picked it up. I ran into the house with it. I unfolded it. First I made sure the story wasn't on the front page. Then I started turning pages. I couldn't find the story! So I turned the pages again, backward, forward. Then I saw it. How could I have missed it the first time? It was easy. I had been looking for my picture. But it wasn't there. Instead there was a big picture of a jar of jelly beans. It didn't look like the jar in the contest, but it was close. It was a dumb picture. Whatever happened to me and my messy room and my cat that the photographer liked so much? I told myself that the film had rotted on

the way back to the newspaper office. What other reason would there be to choose a jar of jelly beans over me?

And there was more bad news. The article was in the "Kids Korner" of the newspaper, along with some cartoons about a nearsighted duck. There was a small square at the top that had YOUTH OF THE MONTH printed right next to the duck. My name was under YOUTH OF THE MONTH, and next to the jelly beans.

I read the article.

JELLY BEANS MELT FORMERLY FIRM FRIENDSHIP

How potent are jelly beans? Beyond being a possible source of dental cavities and a supplier of empty calories, jelly beans have not been recognized as a major cosmic force. Their ability to change the course of lives or to measurably affect human relationships has been uncharted, unacknowledged, and unproven. Until now. According to Frank Kalpal, eleven-year-old honor student at Nathan Clifford Elementary School, jelly beans were breaking up the fast friendship of his pals, Jack Redtress and Lee Goodfellow, also honor students at Nathan Clifford. And Frank was determined to do something about it.

Frank's problem began when Radio Station KNIF ran a How Many Jelly Beans in the Jar? contest at Merry Midtown Mall. Both Jack and Lee guessed 6,666, each claiming to be first with the number. The winning number was 6,931. Since 6,666 was the closest number submitted, Jack and Lee became co-winners, splitting the prize of two tickets to the movie *Monster Mayhem* and all the jelly beans you can eat in two hours. As young Frank explains it, Jack and Lee's friendship was split along with the prize. Frank states that he made numerous attempts to reunite his friends, who, with Frank, are part of a trio known as The Sticky Three.

The articulate fifth grader explains: "I am going to be perfectly Frank. You can put a capital *F* on Frank if you want. But it works both ways, small *f*, big *F*. Well, Jack and Lee wouldn't even speak to each other. All because of jelly beans. Big deal, counting jelly beans! *My* fights, in case you want to know and you probably do, last about fifteen minutes, tops. And they're about important things like dirty names and kicks in the shin. Sometimes the kicks come before the fight, sometimes after. Well, I kept telling Jack and Lee to wise up and be friends again, and now I'm telling them to *stay* friends. Wise up, you guys! And I want to say right here that your newspaper is doing a really terrific job by printing this. You *are* printing this, aren't you?"

In a more relaxed mood, Frank, who plans to enter show business when he grows up, talked about himself. He lives with his parents, Mr. and Mrs. Frank Kalpal, Sr., and one cat, Anastasia Marie, in a comfortable home on a tree-lined street near midtown. He has an extensive and unusual collection of antique soda bottles. He also collects baseball bats as a hobby. "I like sports," Frank enthused, as he deftly smoothed back a stray hair that kept falling over his forehead. Frank has dark hair, merry eyes, and a face that is full of good feeling and optimism. His face brightened as he talked about baseball bats, in marked contrast to his glum expression when he spoke of his friends' fight.

Frank Kalpal, our Youth of the Month. Enterprising, caring, a true friend. May The Sticky Three never again become unglued!

Chapter 17

The article scared me. Except for the picture of the
jelly bean jar instead of me, and describing my hair
(why did she do *that*?) it wasn't a bad write-up—about
me. But what about Jack and Lee? I guess I actually
said those things about them, but it sounded okay *then*.
So why did it look so awful *now*? And what would Jack
and Lee say, and do? To me? Would they know I was
just trying to keep them from having another fight?
Would they know that I did it for them?

And for me. I liked being in the newspaper. I liked
having my name in the newspaper. I liked almost having my picture in the newspaper.

But I should have talked about the camel. That's
how the reporter got interested in me. How many
underage camel importers did she meet in her line of
work? I almost did import that camel. I didn't have

enough money to pay the freight. And my house is a little small. Low ceilings, too.

Now the entire city knew about Jack and Lee's competition. The story was on doorsteps all over town. It was in newspaper vending machines. Someday it would be used to wrap fish and start fires in fireplaces and make paper hats and it would get even more readers as it got rolled up or folded or crushed. As I looked at the article, I knew I had made a big big mistake. I wasn't Youth of the Month. I was Snitch of the Month.

My parents said the article was fine. "The sheriff hasn't come by, and we still have electricity," my mother said. "I'm proud of you, Frank."

All day Sunday I wondered if Jack or Lee would call. I hung around the telephone. But the only calls were from some relatives who also said they were proud of me, and that the newspaper article might get picked up by AP or UPI for national and maybe international publication.

I never thought about that. The jelly bean fight could be translated into a dozen languages. What if they turned it into a major motion picture starring me? *Frank Kalpal, Supersnitch.*

Just before supper, the doorbell rang. I was afraid to answer it, but I didn't want to admit it.

"I'll get it," my mother said as she went to the door. A minute later she came back and gave me an envelope with my name on it. "A girl was at the door," she said. "She didn't say a word. She just handed me this envelope."

I waited until my mother left the room. Then I opened the envelope. A copy of the newspaper article fell out. There was a letter with it, written on stationery that had goats and chickens and pigs and horses and cows marching around the borders. In the upper left-hand corner *Bianca's Barnyard* was printed in brown raised script. There was something about this stationery that I think I was supposed to understand, but I didn't. Bianca was not a member of the 4-H Club and she certainly didn't live in a stable. I read the letter:

Dear Frank,

I saw your jelly bean story in today's newspaper and here is another copy of it in case you want it for an heirloom for your grandchildren. Now I know why you wanted me to be either Jack Redtress's mother or Lee Goodfellow's mother. I have something to tell you. Even if Jack and Lee get very very mad at you for spilling the beans (ha ha), I will always be your sincere and true friend like we talked about that day in the middle of the auditorium. I am writing this down so you can keep it and look at it over and over again because if I just said it, the words might disappear into the air and you would forget that I even said them. So once more—SINCERE AND TRUE FRIEND. But don't get any ideas that I will marry you when we grow up, because Blitz Melnick looks like he is going to ask me. I am making friends all over the place ever since our conversation.

Signing off,

Bianca Wasserman (my autograph)

P.S. Wherever you see a cow on this writing paper, I drew it.

93

The letter cheered me up for about five minutes. I, Frank Kalpal, had inspired warm friendly feelings in Bianca Wasserman. She even drew some cows for me. Jack and Lee must feel the same way about me, but even more so, because they knew me so much better than Bianca did.

But that was the trouble—they knew me so much better!

I put Bianca's letter and the newspaper article back in the envelope. Maybe I would reread the letter now and then. It didn't seem right never to read it again. And besides, I wanted to.

Chapter 18

By nighttime I knew that Jack and Lee weren't going to call. I knew that they would be waiting for me the next day on the way to school.

And now it's the next day. In two and a half minutes I have to leave for school. I think it's a wonderful idea to fly there or dig my way underground.

Maybe I'll stay home today. And for the rest of my life.

No. I always face things. It's part of being Perfectly Frank.

Here I go. Leaving my house. Demolish Frank Time is here.

"Frank!"

Bianca is calling to me. She's cruising by in her family's Cadillac. Her mother is at the wheel.

"Want a ride to school?"

A ride to school! A rescue! I will ride right by Jack and Lee. At school I'll be safe. They won't try to get me on Mr. Sklish's turf. Anyway, I have my day figured out. I will be last into class, and first out of class. I will eat my lunch in a broom closet.

I can't get into the Wasserman Cadillac fast enough. We start up. We're gliding along, smooth and strong in this rescue vehicle. We pass Lee and Jack standing on a corner. They don't see me in the car. That's because I'm ducking.

Bianca's mother says, "Nice article."

"Thanks."

"But it will backfire."

"It will?"

"Yes. It's a disaster."

"A disaster?"

"Full-blown."

"Full-blown?"

"Psychologically invalid."

"Oh."

"You meant well. Not everyone has a friend like you."

Bianca giggles.

"I'm glad that Bianca found you. You're just what she needs."

Bianca half covers her face. I think she *loves* me. I'll deal with that later.

At school Bianca's mother parks the car and walks in with us! What does it mean? With Bianca's mother, it must mean something.

She smiles. "I'm attending school today. It's Community Day, you know. I'm going to give a talk about being a psychologist."

I had forgotten about Community Day. People who do things for others in the community come to the school and talk about their contributions. All the students are invited to the auditorium to listen.

Good. Jack and Lee won't try to get me in front of all those people.

Bianca's mother leaves us. "See you later," she says as she heads for Mr. Sklish's office.

Bianca and I go to the auditorium. We're early. We have our choice of seats.

"I want to sit in the front row so I can see my mother better," she explains.

"I prefer the back row."

"I know why. But the front row is better. Kids get away with things in the back row, if you know what I mean."

I know what she means. The front row it is.

The auditorium starts to fill up. I hunch over into my front-row seat and put my hands around my eyes as if it's too sunny in the room. I don't turn around.

Bianca turns around for me. "Jack and Lee are five rows in back of us," she reports.

I look at the stage. There are nine empty chairs in a row, and a banner with the words COMMUNITY DAY. Mr. Sklish suddenly appears in front of the banner at a mike. He begins to speak. He says he wants to extend a special thanks to "all those children who asked these community stars to be with us today."

The star people file onto the stage. Bianca's mother is first. Bianca applauds, so everybody does. There are nine guests up there. They sit down in the chairs. One of them, a tall man, looks familiar, but I can't figure out why.

I'm thinking about the game Musical Chairs. There are nine chairs up there and ten people. Every time a community person gets up to speak, Mr. Sklish will have to sit in that person's chair, or else he'll have to stand through nine speeches. You'd think he'd have his own chair.

Bianca's mother is the first speaker. Mr. Sklish introduces her. "Dr. Glinka Wasserman, one of this community's outstanding psychologists."

Bianca's mother gets up and goes to the mike. Mr. Sklish leaves the mike and takes the vacant chair. I bet it's still warm.

Bianca's mother has plenty to say. That doesn't surprise me. What surprises me is that she seems to be making sense. She talks about her patients and their problems and how she tries to help people. She says that each person has a little piece of territory in life, and should be in charge of his or her own territory. Then she says that each of us is different from everyone else, and that makes life richer. Then she tells us to look at the persons on both sides of us (unless we're sitting against a wall—ha ha) and notice how each is unique.

Bianca is on my right and I've already seen her. I hate to change my hunched-over position to look to the left of me. But I do. Lemon Derringer is sitting there!

She's there on purpose, I know it. She smiles at me. *Yuck!* She's after me again. I must be Lemon's one and

98

only hobby. She works at her hobby as hard as I work at being Perfectly Frank. Perfectly Lemon. It fits.

Bianca's mother is talking about "human behavior," and now I'm getting some ideas of my own on this subject. I'm beginning to wonder if Lemon likes me and that's why she acts like she doesn't. How can you hate a person as much as she hates me without liking that person? Should I ask Bianca's mother? She's taking questions from the audience. What if I tried being a friend to Lemon Derringer. A friend to Lemon Derringer? Let's not get carried away.

It's strange, though. The three of us are sitting here and I'm part of a trio again. I'm between two girls and I'm feeling popular. They're sitting here because I'm here. Like they're interested in *my* territory. It makes me feel important. I wish they'd get up and fight over me.

Bianca's mother gets lots of applause as she leaves the mike. I clap for her too. She doesn't look like she was ever Mrs. Slime Who Ate Cleveland.

Mr. Sklish thanks her for giving us her "valuable time and insights." Then he says, "One of the finest aspects of Community Day is the variety of services we explore. Our next speaker is from the world of animals. He knows virtually all there is to know about pets, so listen to him carefully and you might even pick up a tip about *your* pet."

A veterinarian. I could ask him about Anastasia Marie's shedding.

The tall man who looks familiar starts to get up from his chair as Mr. Sklish introduces him. "A friend to

99

animals, a friend to us, Mr. Rigby Damson, owner of the Merry Midtown Mall International Pet Store!"

No! It's the man who described me as "the boy with the ferret eyes." It's the man who sold me Mildred the Riot Gerbil. He seems to be looking straight at me.

Lemon nudges me. "*I* brought him," she says. "After everyone's finished, I'm going to introduce you to Mr. Damson right in front of Mr. Sklish." Lemon's eyes are wild with happiness. "Unless," she adds, "you two have already met."

Lemon never gives up! She reminds me of somebody. *Me.* I remember how she described my schemes: "Major, colossal, stupendous." That was praise, that's what it was. I now understand Lemon Derringer, and it terrifies me. I am her role model. She envies me. She wants to be like me. She *wants* to be Perfectly Lemon. She's not only after me, she's my competition.

I have to leave!

We're allowed to leave the auditorium to go to the bathroom. We can just get up silently, leave, and come back silently.

I whisper to Bianca, "Your mother's speech was super," and I get up and walk away before she knows what's happening. I hope Lemon isn't following me. I don't want to turn around and find out. It's a long walk to the door. Eyes are on me, I know it. Jack's. Lee's. The student body's. Mr. Damson from the pet store is probably asking himself, "Is he or isn't he?" The story about me was in yesterday's newspaper and I feel much too famous. I feel like I'm *on* stage instead of slinking out past it.

I'm thinking of a new contest for Jack and Lee.

100

Compute the distance between where I was sitting and the door of the auditorium. And the answer is . . . Three thousand miles, not a mile less.

The longest walk Frank Kalpal ever took is over. I am outside the auditorium now. Now it's time for the longest run.

But I don't move. I can't. I can't run away from this. I'm going to turn around and face Jack and Lee. I'm going to face the entire school, because that's the way I am.

I open the door to the auditorium, I walk back inside, and then I turn and walk right up onto the stage!

Mr. Damson, the pet store owner, is nervously answering pet questions. He turns and looks at me. He doesn't recognize me. He is answering a question from a kid: "Can you overpat your dog? Will it wear him out?"

"I doubt it," says Mr. Damson, and he goes back to his chair before he can be asked any more stupid questions.

Mr. Sklish, who had been sitting in Mr. Damson's chair, has to get up.

I grab the mike. It's higher than I am. I face the audience. "I'm a community service person too. I try to help others. Sometimes I succeed, sometimes I fall flat on my face. Let me explain myself."

Mr. Sklish walks up to me. "You're not on the program, Frank. We don't have a chair for you."

I had spoiled his plan for there always to be a seat for him.

Bianca's mother stands up. "You can have mine, Frank."

She's really a nice lady. The city of Cleveland should be proud to be eaten by her. I give her a big smile.

"Thanks, but I just have something brief to say and then I'll leave." I turn back to the mike.

"I have to introduce you, Frank," Mr. Sklish says. "That's the way this program is arranged. Unfortunately, words fail me."

"You don't have to introduce me. Everybody knows me. That's part of my trouble." I stretch up and talk into the mike. "As I was saying, I *try*."

Mr. Sklish interrupts. "We're happy that you try, Frank, and now I'd like to introduce—"

"But—"

"A big hand for Frank Kalpal for trying," Mr. Sklish says as he kind of shoves me away from the mike. "Frank is our budding paper clip champ. A big hand for this ambitious young man."

Bianca stands up and cheers. Some other kids stand up. I'm looking for Jack and Lee but I can't see them. I get some hoots. I get some whistles. I get some applause.

I have to get used to this, I guess. When I grow up and enter show business I'll be dealing with all kinds of audiences. I hear that they throw cream pies and rotten tomatoes at you if they don't like you.

Should I take a bow? Maybe not. Mr. Sklish looks mad. The audience is getting noisier and noisier.

I leave the stage. I walk out of the auditorium, as Mr. Sklish yells "QUIET!"

102

Outside the auditorium I stop and lean against a wall. I hope I haven't wrecked Community Day. I don't think I should hang around and find out.

I run.

Chapter 19

I run around a corner. And another corner. Then I
stop and lean against a wall. Free!

Not free. I hear running feet. I peer back around
the corner. The feet belong to Jack and Lee. I start to
run again. Then I stop.

Why am I running? These are my friends. We've
always been friends. They've always understood my
being Perfectly Frank. But now I'm asking myself . . .
have I understood *them*? Everybody has his or her own
little piece of territory. That's what Bianca's mother
said. Maybe I invaded their territory. If I hadn't made
a big deal out of that jelly bean contest, it wouldn't
have been a big deal.

I turn around and wait for them. Now the three of
us are back together again, so to speak.

Jack glares at me. "Frank, you went too far this time.

The entire city knows about our fight, thanks to you. Why did you do that? Lee and I are friends. You *know* that!"

"But for how long? What about the newspaper contest?"

Lee makes a face. "We decided we don't like to read *The Arizona Daily Times*. Not even twenty-five words' worth."

"Yeah," said Jack. "Especially now."

I shift my feet. "You both hate me, right?"

"No," says Lee.

"How about mildly dislike?"

"You're getting close," says Jack.

"Maybe you think I'm wonderful? For trying to help you?"

"Whoa!" says Lee. "Back up all the way to mildly dislike and stay there."

"Look, guys. I admit I used to play pranks. I started small. Salt in sugar bowls. Underwear on flagpoles. Then I advanced to naked baby pictures and secret admirers. But this newspaper thing was supposed to be different. I was trying to help you. I didn't mean to invade your territory."

"Our territory? You heard that fifteen minutes ago," said Jack. "What would you have said to us *before* the assembly?"

"That the words *jelly beans* never should have left my lips."

"Good thinking," says Jack.

I look at each of them. "Let's be friends again, *please*."

Jack and Lee have these strange expressions on their

105

faces. And smiles that I'd never seen before and hope never to see again.

"Okay, we're still friends," Jack says to me. Just like that.

And Lee nods his head yes.

I'm feeling grateful and gushy. "You guys are just—fantastic!"

"No, we're not," says Jack.

Jack is a very humble person.

Chapter 20

Jack is not a very humble person.

He meant it when he said that he and Lee are not fantastic. And I think they are about to prove it. Don't get me wrong. We *are* pals again, Jack, Lee, and me. A week has gone by and The Sticky Three are hanging around together and going places together. Except for one place. Radio Station KNIF. Jack and Lee are going on radio. Without me. Tasha and Daddy-O invited them to go on a local news program and talk about the jelly bean business and their friend Frank. They read my newspaper story and told Jack and Lee that they deserved "equal time" to talk about me. This is another of Tasha's and Daddy-O's demented plans. I can just see Tasha licking her chops, hoping that the identity of the Rodent Releaser will finally be broadcast over the KNIF airwaves. I'm sure that the name Frank Kalpal is now at the top of her list of suspects. And under my name are a lot of ditto marks.

I thought that Jack and Lee wanted to forget all about the contest, that they wanted to move forward, not backward. But maybe they have to move backward before they can move forward.

I'm moving backward too. I'm remembering the look Lee gave me when he saw his naked baby picture on the bulletin board. And the look Jack gave me when he saw I was his secret admirer. But most of all I remember the way both of them looked at me when Jack told me they were not fantastic.

Speaking of backward, I just noticed what KNIF spells backward.

Jack and Lee are going on the radio in five minutes. Yesterday I asked them what they are going to say about me. They smiled a little fiendishly and said they are going to be "perfectly frank."

I hope the principal won't be tuned in. He'll toss his paper clips into the air and cry, *"Proof! After all these years, I've got Proof!"*

Then he'll dance around the room with Lemon Derringer.

Dr. Slime will try to readopt me.

But they can't stop me. Nobody can.

Right now I've got a great new idea I'm itching to use if I can just get everything together. All I need is some ticker tape, fifteen stalks of celery, and the governor of the state.

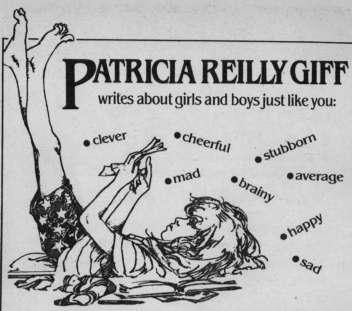

PATRICIA REILLY GIFF

writes about girls and boys just like you:

- clever
- cheerful
- stubborn
- mad
- brainy
- average
- happy
- sad

Show your parents this list of her funny, serious, wonderful books
—to own, read, and treasure for years!

_____ FOURTH GRADE CELEBRITY	42676-6	$2.25
_____ GIFT OF THE PIRATE QUEEN	43046-1	2.25
_____ THE GIRL WHO KNEW IT ALL	42855-6	2.50
_____ HAVE YOU SEEN HYACINTH MACAW?	43450-5	2.50
_____ LEFT-HANDED SHORTSTOP	44672-4	2.25
_____ LORETTA P. SWEENY, WHERE ARE YOU?	44926-X	2.25
_____ THE WINTER WORM BUSINESS	49259-9	2.50

Yearling Books

At your local bookstore or use this handy coupon for ordering:

 DELL READERS SERVICE—DEPT. B859B
P.O. BOX 1000, PINE BROOK, N.J. 07058

Please send me the above title(s). I am enclosing $_____ (please add 75¢ per copy to cover postage and handling). Send check or money order—no cash or COOs. Please allow 3-4 weeks for shipment. CANADIAN ORDERS: please submit in U.S. dollars.

Ms./Mrs./Mr _____

Address_____

City/State_____ Zip_____

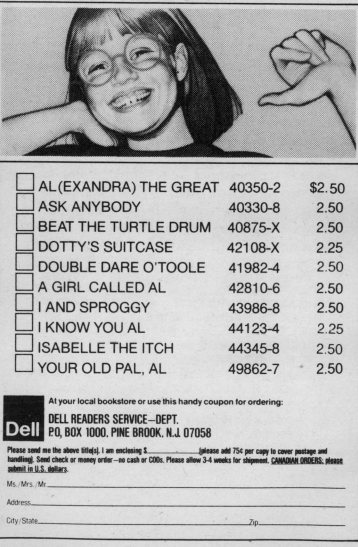